HERMIT CRAB'S HOME
Safe in a Shell

SMITHSONIAN OCEANIC COLLECTION

With love to my daughter Pam, who has always felt the call of the water.—J.H.

To my father, George T. Harrington.—D.B.

Book copyright © 2007 Trudy Corporation and the Smithsonian Institution, Washington, DC 20560.

Published by Soundprints, an imprint of Trudy Corporation, Norwalk, Connecticut.

Series design: Shields & Partners, Westport, CT
Book layout: Bert Johnstone
Editor: Barbie Heit Schwaeber

First Edition 2007
10 9 8 7 6 5 4 3 2 1
Printed in China

Acknowledgments:
    Our very special thanks to Dr. Raphael Lemaitre of the Department of Vertebrate Zoology at the Smithsonian Institution's National Museum of Natural History for his curatorial review.
    Soundprints would like to thank Ellen Nanney at the Smithsonian Institution's Office of Product Development and Licensing for her help in the creation of this book.

HERMIT CRAB'S HOME
Safe in a Shell

by Janet Halfmann   Illustrated by Bob Dacey & Debra Bandelin

4

Splash! The clear blue waters of the Caribbean Sea wash over a tiny egg tossed onto the seashore rocks by a mother land hermit crab. Out pops a baby, no bigger than a tiny dot. She floats out into the wide open sea.

For weeks, the tiny baby drifts, eating even tinier animals and plants. With bulging eyes and a long shrimp-like body, she looks nothing like her mother.

The baby keeps growing and changing. Finally, she begins to look something like a hermit crab, with tiny claws, eyes on stalks and red walking legs. Now, she sinks to the floor of the sea near the shore.

7

A hungry fish tries to nip her soft tail end. She needs an empty snail shell for protection—and FAST. She spots a tiny checkered nerite shell and tucks her rear into it. It's a perfect fit. Now, she's safe in her first shell home.

9

10

But this baby hermit crab still has much more changing to do.
One night, she crawls onto a white, sandy beach in the Virgin Islands.
She wanders for a while, then burrows into the wet sand.

When she digs out days later, she has finally changed into a young land
hermit crab, with a big left claw and special gills for breathing on land.
She crawls away from the sea to live in the forest behind the beach.

11

In the daytime heat, she hides under shady tree roots or joins other land hermit crabs in a hollow tree stump. Using her big purple claw as a door, she blocks the opening of her shell. Inside, she stays cool, moist and out of sight. Hungry gulls soaring overhead don't even notice her.

13

As the sun sets, cooling the air, she scuttles into the open. She's thirsty. Waggling her feelers, she soon finds a freshwater pond. She dips her claws in, drinks the cool water and fills her shell to wet her gills.

Wiggle, waggle. Now, her feelers smell food—fallen fruit, dead fish, insects and animal waste. Scurrying up a trunk, she devours a poison apple from the Manchineel tree, but it doesn't hurt her one bit.

14

16

One night, she stops eating. Her skin has gotten too tight for her body. *Dig, dig, dig.* She digs into the moist soil and disappears. Safe in her hiding place, her skin splits and she wriggles free.

Now she's soft and squishy, with a new, larger skin. Puffing herself up with water, she grows bigger, then eats her old skin to help her new one harden. When she's ready, *dig, dig, dig.* Out she comes, ready to eat again.

But wait! Her body is bigger, so now her shell is too small. She needs to find a new home.

Before long, her googly eyes spot the pretty shell of a tree snail. Rolling it over, she looks inside. Surprise! A snail is still living in it.

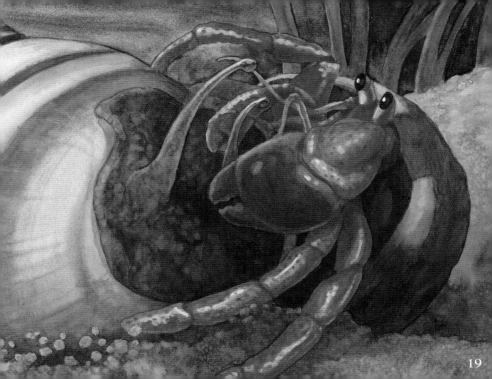

19

Searching some more, she spies a conch shell poking out from a clump of sea grass high on the beach. As she measures the big shell, the shadow of a galloping ghost crab startles her. Quickly, she ducks into the roomy shell.

She waits for the shadow to pass, then tries to walk. She can't even move. The shell is too heavy! Luckily, no other hermit crab took her old shell, and she quickly darts back into it.

A little farther down the beach, she tumbles over the walls of a big sand castle built earlier that day by Ashley and Sean, friends who are visiting the island. What's that perched on top of the castle's highest tower? It looks like a toy spinning top, but it's a West Indian top shell.

Land Hermit Crab measures the shell's round opening. She lifts it. She taps its smooth, pearly inside. Quickly she backs in. It is a perfect fit! Finally, she has a new home.

Early the next morning, Ashley and Sean come back to check on their castle. They find an odd pattern of footprints all over it, and their favorite seashell is missing!

The friends search higher up the beach under a coconut palm where they find Land Hermit Crab tightly tucked into the black-and-white top shell. They gently lift the shell, examine the creature inside, then carefully return Land Hermit Crab to her shady resting spot.

25

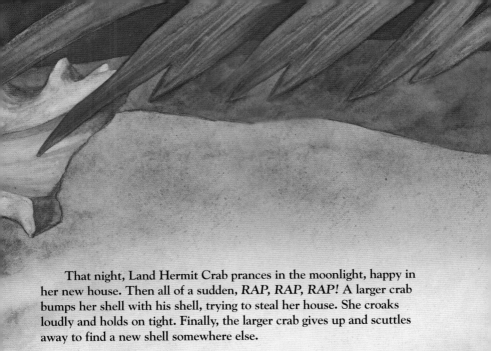

That night, Land Hermit Crab prances in the moonlight, happy in her new house. Then all of a sudden, *RAP, RAP, RAP!* A larger crab bumps her shell with his shell, trying to steal her house. She croaks loudly and holds on tight. Finally, the larger crab gives up and scuttles away to find a new shell somewhere else.

27

The months pass and Land Hermit Crab is now almost two years old. On an August night just before the full moon, she heads toward the sea. Thousands of land hermit crabs march with her, their shells clattering together in the night.

Near the sea, she mates with a male crab and lays hundreds of eggs. She attaches them to her body, keeping them safe and moist inside her shell. The male crab returns to his home in the beach forest.

28

29

A few weeks later, Land Hermit Crab and the other females rush to the sea to toss their light blue eggs onto wet rocks near the water's edge. Then, when their job is done, they head back home.

Later, the high tide waters rush in, and pop! Thousands of tiny babies float into the wide, open sea. In a couple of months, many of them will crawl ashore, wearing tiny seashells, to start their lives as land hermit crabs.

30

About the Land Hermit Crab

The land hermit crab belongs to a small family of hermit crabs that live most of their lives on land. Most species of hermit crabs li[ve] sea. Hermit crabs differ from other crabs by not having hard shells covering their entire bodies. The long back part, or abdomen, of a h[e] sticks out, unprotected. To keep this soft part safe, a hermit crab wears the abandoned shell of a dead land or sea snail.

This borrowed shell also helps the land hermit crab live on land. The crab carries a supply of water in its shell to keep its gills and moist, so it can breathe. Its shell covering also keeps moisture in, so the crab doesn't dry out. The land hermit crab hides during the day at night when the air is cool and moist. It lives among plants above the beach, as far as two miles from the shore.

Although land hermit crabs live on land, they must return to the sea to release their eggs. The seawater makes the eggs hatch. Th[ey] shed their skins, or molt, going through several growth stages, before they crawl onto land. Land hermit crabs continue to molt through[out] lives. The land hermit crab is known by many other common names, including soldier crab, purple pincher crab and tree crab. Its scien[tific] is *Coenobita clypeatus*. It is native to the warm shores of the western Atlantic and Caribbean, from southern Florida to Venezuela.

The land hermit crab is a popular pet in the United States and elsewhere. Since it lives on land, it is much easier to care for than hermit crab. The land hermit crab likes company, so pet owners often keep more than one. The crab is about 1-1/2 inches long and ca[n] years or more.

Glossary

checkered nerite: Small sea snail.
coconut palm: Tall tree with large feathery leaves and coconut fruits.
conch: Large sea snail.
feelers: Sense organs used to smell, taste and feel; also called antennae.
freshwater: Water that is not salty.
gills: Organs for taking oxygen from water.
ghost crab: Swift, sand-colored land crab that lives in burrows.
high tide: The waters that cover the greatest area of the shore.
Manchineel tree: Tree with green, apple-like fruits that are poisonous to people but not to the land hermit crab.
snail: Animal that has a soft body protected by a spiral shell. A snail is a mollusk. Some species live on land, others in the water.
West Indian top shell: Shell of a sea snail often used by the land hermit crab.